AF091941

WHISPERS FROM ABOVE

Victoria Nilsen

Author's Tranquility Press
ATLANTA, GEORGIA

Copyright © 2024 by VICTORIA NILSEN

All rights reserved. No part of this publication may be reproduced, distributed or transmitted in any form or by any means, including photocopying, recording, or other electronic or mechanical methods, without the prior written permission of the publisher, except in the case of brief quotations embodied in critical reviews and certain other noncommercial uses permitted by copyright law. For permission requests, write to the publisher, addressed "Attention: Permissions Coordinator," at the address below.

VICTORIA NILSEN/Author's Tranquility Press
3900 N Commerce Dr. Suite 300 #1255
Atlanta, GA 30344
www.authorstranquilitypress.com

Ordering Information:
Quantity sales. Special discounts are available on quantity purchases by corporations, associations, and others. For details, contact the "Special Sales Department" at the address above.

WHISPERS FROM ABOVE/VICTORIA NILSEN
Paperback: 978-1-962859-84-4
eBook: 978-1-962859-82-0

There are special people
They crowd the sun when it's sunrise.
And they shine in my heart first.
Their noise is joyful and joyful.
Their morning is the most beautiful presence in life.
I find myself every morning.
I choose the best words for them, which I like.
I write it down for them in the sweetest lines.
Your morning is as white as your heart.
morning Roses and Jasmine

Peace be upon the letters to say.
She is the one who reported what was said.
Peace be upon those who remain silent.
Within cities of speech
Peace be upon those who possess the innocence of hearts.
In a time when feelings were honored
Peace be upon the good and pure hearts that bear fruit in love.
It gives us hope in life.
For those who have the beauty of the soul
And the purity of intention, and their hearts do not know anything but loyalty

For me, this is something that does not break my heart or anything. When I feel the energy of love, I also give my energy to love for others, because I love the world, I love people, I love life, but I love love itself.

Increase my love for love, if it kills me, then revives me. I am the oldest capital of love.

I offer the capital of love, and my wound is a pharaonic inscription, and my pain extends like a flock of pigeons from Baghdad to China. Increase me in love, O woman. If you kill me, you will revive me.

O dearest woman among the women of the universe, hold me.

O you who loved you until love burned, love me, if you want to live, I will live in you in the light of my eyes.

Your love is my map, and the map of the world no longer concerns me.

Here I am, from the beginning of my formative years, looking for a homeland that will strengthen me, find the bosom of a woman, take me to the limits of the sun, and throw me away.

They said that you live with her, of course. They said that you stay up with her, of course. Of course, her eyes are my house, my bed, and the pillow of my head. Her ribs erase the worries of my life.

Erase the worries of my life from me. If her finger prostrates me, hold me, dearest woman. If I remain silent, my heart can hear her.

O sincere heart and beautiful soul, life is sweeter than everything. Live the moment, live life, live your day as you want, do what you love. This life is for everyone to live in it with love, love, love, love

They blame me for my love for you, and they say how do you love her, and she was not yours and never will be yours.

And I tell them how you breathe, and you know that you will die. Love is a gift from God not in our hands. Someone to forget, whoever loves sincerely will never forget a heart that lived by it and lived for it, so he loved life, I loved your soul, so I interpreted you as a lover, I love life, I will always love you, and your love will remain eternal as long as I live in life, I love everything about you. Your voice whispered your name. This is your breath. I loved passion I loved life Oh a dream I lived wishing for and if the world separates us and a million oh in my heart I will not give up on your love And I will not forget it I will live with a heart that reminds you And Sansa remembers you the worries of life When I remember your kindness Smile and forget the worries of life.

The most expensive things are those that money cannot buy:

Wellness in the body, peace of mind, and people who make it easy.

You have the world. Not every relationship between two people is love.

There are people whose words we feel comfortable with because they touch our reality.

And people whose ideas we love because they give us a spirit of hope and challenge.

And people we love because they make us happy with their smile.

As for love, it is something that touches the heart and is felt by the soul.

And preoccupied with thought and congratulations to those who beat him.

The heart and the soul feel it and misses it
It engages our mind.
You are misunderstood by people sometimes.
They create descriptions for you in colors.
You may be an angel to some of them
In some people's eyes, it may be a demon
People's natures are diverse and they are moods
You will not be able to understand it
"Do not be deceived by praise if they come to you
No slander will harm you, no matter what
The soul does not know a person like its owner
"Be a balance for yourself in the evaluation

Don't leave someone who likes to talk to you; You don't know who you are with him, you may be the only one left for him or everything for him.

When you finish your conversation with the one you love, delete it, do not ask about the reason, within the days you will know.

There are no absurd encounters in life, every person you encounter is either a test, a punishment, or a gift from heaven.

If you are praying and time is not enough for you and your needs are crowded in your heart, then make all your supplications that God will forgive you.

The departure of something forever is much easier than living in the hope that it will return and not return.

Perhaps you do not know that someone is speaking to God.

For your sake now.

Do not think that the calmness that you see in your face indicates contentment, for every person has something inside him that shakes him and torments him.

Motivational advice

For the second, third, and millionth time, beware, beware of fearing something before it happens, do not imagine, divert your thoughts and fear from the unseen, for they are in the knowledge of God. And know that if affliction descends upon a servant, kindness descends with him, so if you imagine the affliction before it occurs, then you have received the affliction without kindness and perished. Your soul, it is your duty to be certain that you have a God who is omnipotent and does not sleep, so rest assured of Him, trust in Him, be optimistic, and be optimistic about goodness.

People believe that it is like a soul.

He's someone who's perfect for us, and that's what they want, but a true soulmate is a mirror. Someone who shows you everything inside of you so you can change your life.

A true soul-like is perhaps the most important person you will ever meet because he will push your limits, tear down your walls, and wake you up. The most beautiful gifts in life are not things, but people. The likeness of a thing attracted to it is not the likeness of a soul.

So, God, choose for us hearts that are similar to our hearts, and do not choose us, in my heart a large space.

He is preoccupied with small details that do not attract many, such as the smell of the earth after the rain, a small child who stumbled in his gait as he came to hug me from among those sitting, or a fleeting reading of someone's phrases describing a feeling that I was unable to understand.

The moment of understanding itself is special, when dark thoughts in my head suddenly light up and I realize things in a more comprehensive way. They are all very simple things, but they touch my heart easily and restore the flow of happiness in it.

When a person is in touch with his heart, you will instantly fall in love with him, the moment you see him, you will fall in love with him. You don't know why he has such sweetness about it. That sweetness your mind may not be able to detect, but your heart detects it instantly. He has an aura.

The moment you come into his aura you are drunk. You feel the longing for him, you feel the attraction, a magnetic force at work. You may not be aware of what is happening; You might simply say.

"I don't know why I'm drawn," but here's the reason".

The person whose heart lives in has sweetness around him, sweetness flows around him. You are drowning in it whenever you are in contact with this person.

Finally, I greet you with the greeting of Islam, may God's peace, mercy and blessings be upon you. It begins with peace, in the middle is mercy, and at the end is blessing.

Liebe verkürzt Entfernungen, Alter und Zeiten, und dass man einen Menschen trifft und einmal mit ihm zusammensitzt; Und er wird mit deinem Geist verbunden sein, als ob du im Wissen die Kinder eines Hauses wärst; Die Seele ist zu Hause und das Herz ist zu Hause!

Charm???

It is not magic and certainly not human.
He is a unique individual who shines like the moon.
He is a stubborn light who does not accept bans.
He is great, lonely, and does not tend to look at others.
He dwells in the folds of the heart, playing on every string.
A melody of Sarmadi love, a fire that left embers in my heart.
He runs away and suddenly disappears without a trace.
And when I forget him, I see him knocking the mosquito of danger.
The fugitive has returned. Do not try to forget him.
There is no escape from returning to him.
The sword of his love Buridi was slaughtered.
No matter how much I try to turn and turn and return to Him helplessly, without strength, without thought.

And our situation remains in the hands of God. May our union be approved.

A stalker congratulates his escape, wounds from memories heal, and joy on the board of their time, digging holes with love.

She said,
Who are you, how did you float in my stars?
And why did I accept you to be orphaned.

I didn't know what passion and passion are,
Before you come and live in my blood

I noticed that I was lying asleep, but it was not.
My heart to you is a wanderer or in love.

Until you came and became all my stories
You lived in my heart and became my teacher.
She said and your voice does not leave my ears.
And its echo makes me happy, and I sing in it.

How high I would be if your spectrum visited my mind.
And I shall have a chain around my wrist.

Since I knew you, fugitives have got me lost.
Oh you, my beautiful medicine and my balm.
And your love made me drunk and did not have mercy on me.

How you forcibly stormed the castles of my heart.
My heart is stubborn and never gives up.
So, I came obediently leading me.
She said, kissing you with passion, I did not dream.

My thoughts are lost in you, my selfishness and confusion.
Oh, the sweetest names my mouth utters.
She said I love you like this despite the intentions.

We may meet one day, and you will be my twin.

What is the lineage of the soul? Each of us has the apparent lineage, but the lineage of the soul is the lineage of myself.

So, the soul is God's gift to worship those close to him, to communicate with him, and it is the door to the servant's entry into the station of charity. Attributing the soul is one of the unseen matters that you only perceive through the path of behavior to God, so it was revealed by revelations and observations, and meanings and radiances were revealed to him, and his lineage was revealed to him. The "righteous." And we are the earth, so the inheritance of the righteous is the inheritance of an honorable prophetic, so they are the ones of whom Allah said,

"God has testified that there is no God, he and the angels, and the people of knowledge."

Because they are knowledgeable, the righteous are the scholars who are the heirs of the prophets, and Allah has singled them out for spiritual guidance from time immemorial. Two orphaned boys in the city, and under it there was a treasure for them.

"I will go back to my treasure, I will go back to my treasure, and I will go out to your treasure, as a mercy from your Lord."

In honor of this righteous person, Allah sent a prophet of determination, who is Moses and Al-Khidr, who is the Spirit.

Peace be upon him, to keep that treasure for them under heavy guard from Allah. For every boy who has a good father (a spiritual father), God has preserved for you a treasure with a heavy guard that is greater by destroying the wall of yourself with behavior, purification, and integrity. The treasure is (the treasure of divine knowledge) And thank God, Lord of the worlds.

A phrase I don't like, the phrase says stay for the strongest. I say no, stay for the most loyal, for the best, for the most honest, for the purest, the true survival of the one who carries in his heart a smile, and in his mind affection, and in his feelings the mercy of survival for those who have humanity in his actions and love in him. His dealings and tenderness in his behavior, "Stay for those who guide you for help for free and for those who carry the burdens of life without the goal of staying for sweet feelings, pure intentions and merciful hearts".

What is the meaning of the case?

The condition is a garment that is thrown from the soul on its owner, so he is not the owner of it, nor is he leaving it.

And the meaning…

For those who remember God a lot, and for women, there are lights, and those lights provide the soul with their strength, and those strong have an attribute, and that attribute is the cloak.

And what is meant is that he is not his owner, that is. He has no business in his capacity, nor is he leaving him, that is, he is not allowed to change it at will.

When the remembrance is mentioned with purity, the Lord of Glory reminds them of His attribute, and then that attribute is what provides the soul with its light, and the matter of that light is the matter of the attribute.

And among the people is he who claims conditions, so he is like the thief of the garment, taking the form of the garment, but without the light of the attribute, and thank Allah the god of everything.

The secret of the soul

Whoever loves a woman for her soul, let the love last forever. Because the soul lasts forever as for the love of the body. The body annihilates and dies.

If someone looks at you,

"coldly" because you own the "blanket."
"crying" because you carry a "handkerchief."
"In pain" because you put the "bandage" on

With panic and fear, because you revealed that.
I hope you have psychological comfort.
Enthusiasm because you have the sparkle, with ambiguity and Suspicion because you have Complicity.
In turmoil because you have love.
Therefore, no one comes to you by chance everything has a reason.

The luminous female
They will call you.
They will ask and they will look for you.

They will wish to accompany you and sit with you, even for a few seconds to absorb your energy.

Be careful, be smart, follow your sense and intuition. Listen to the voice of your soul, the voice of your guides, the voice of light that is always in contact with you. That voice will not let you down, the voice of your divine self.

Close your aura, keep healing, love yourself and make me your principle first.
My peace of mind first.
Stay away from polluted auras, your light is tempting them, and your energy is the reason they revolve around you.
You are a treasure; they have always drained and live off your cosmic gifts.
The road is long to recovery, raise your worth, seek divine support and receive gifts.

Only you deserve it, and when you heal your soul will automatically overflow with unconditional love and light for the entire universe without waiting for anything in return.

A person can write beautiful words of love, but the most beautiful thing about love is not words, but situations. Love is a ray of light that fate has dropped in the heart, it refuses to leave; forgetting refuses to be rust or corrosion with time. It is a soul that inhabits us and souls never grow old or gray.

So, congratulations to everyone who appreciated the meaning of love and an excuse for those who lived to represent it.

Love is not valued in all its meanings, words from the heart.

Don't think of anything,

Just from your first moments waking up in the morning, look at the light of the sun as it rises to the whisper of the morning light to all the atoms of the universe.

Breathe in it, feel this radiance and its atoms of light. Breathe deeply….

Inhale the scent of nature, flowers, trees, roses, water, air and sky.

To the birds chirping with their cosmic joy.

Just look with deep contemplation of this universal tenderness and beauty that exists in abundance.

Look at yourself, you are in existence.

It is an outpouring of God's abundance, generosity, giving, and unlimited satisfaction.

It's gentle breezes that penetrate all our pores refresh the soul, body, mind and entity.

Do not think about anything, just enter this world of unlimited beauty, peace, harmony and cosmic harmony. Then you will

realize the greatness of blessings and the grace of existence in everything.

We will be grateful for our existence, the light itself, the light…

Just don't think of anything, grateful, grateful and grateful for the overflow of cosmic happiness with every atom.

This is us and this is here and now, live the moment. The light for you is in his presence, your presence, the unconditional love with all submission, satisfaction and acceptance.

I'm on a temporary visit to Earth. I don't have time for arguments, quarrels and revenge. There is no time for hatred, malice, malice and envy. I don't care who said, who did, or who arrived, I came alone, and I will return alone, and I am the only one responsible for my experience.

I came to sip from the love and beauty of this land and what is on it. To learn, to laugh and cry, to enjoy and toil, to taste, to smell, to watch, to play, to dance, to sing, to jump, to fly, to meditate, to travel, to love and adore.

Drawing the heart itself, so it embraced the cosmic whole with its holy triangle.

The veins from it made their way through the structure of life, so they pulsated with the flower and its fragrance, and the arteries od the abdominals flowed, so the heart, embraced by love, became a cosmic body with its spiritual love shining with existence.

Not with the eyes we see our loved ones, it is the heart to doubt it. The eyes see you in different forms. There are those who see you with the eyes of beauty and there are those who see you with the eyes of morals. There are those who see you with appreciation and respect. But there is an eye that sees the beauty of it all, maybe more…

It is the eye of the heart; this is how we see loved ones.

Affection and love are close to hearts and souls, not bodies.

How beautiful it is to be a source of confidence and comfort for people, they only know you through your words.

We may meet souls and not be able to see their features.

We may love words that touch our hearts without knowing who wrote them.

We may cry with eyes that our eyes did not see, and we may rejoice for the joy of hearts whose smiles were scattered letters. Respect for the soul remains the highest title of love.

If we love the soul, then the soul does not perish but if we love the body then the body is mortal. Because the love of the soul has no other, but the love of the body perishes with the days.

How do you look for?

To find you and start your way, the beginning of the search first is within you.

Sit with you constantly and review yourself.

Make your past day a reference for the present.

Make your present day a reference for the future.

Do not begin to blame anyone until you obtain in acquittal from him and after obtaining the clearance for you, you must search for the clearance for the person you want to blame.

Do not pass judgement on yourself or others except after conducting a deliberation between your mind and your heart and excluding yourself in it.

See time as you, every moment you don't see your true self is a waste of time

Soul love is one of the strongest types of love. Where there is no meeting, no end, and no departure.

A complex philosophy and a unique case that he realizes.
The two without revelation, love can.
He leaves the heart but does not leave the soul.
Herein lies the difficulty lover soul.
He has no greed where there is no meeting or saturation.
He who loves the soul does not care about the body.
The shape is as long as the love of the soul is sufficient.
Even if there is no meeting.
Soul lovers are the purest human beings inhabit the earth.

You will continue to resist and resist until your sad mask falls, and your weakness is revealed. But only in front of the one you see who is the most able to contain it, perhaps because he also went through what you suffer.

You will continue to struggle to make everyone happy, but no one will see behind the scenes of your smile except a person who sees you with his heart before his eyes, and only then will you realize what it means for someone to represent the whole world to you.

The soul tends to those who look like it, and the heart tends to those who enter it without permission.
God distributes his love among humans as he pleases, and souls of all kinds meet.

The language of the soul makes no mistakes, and the memory of the soul is unforgettable. The strength of the spirit is indomitable.

The beauty of the soul is indescribable.

The love of the soul never ends.

The soul, if possessed, filled if you doubt and if you like, live.

All we need is,

We need someone to send peace to our souls while we are at the height of distress.

We need someone to remove the fog of hallucinations from us so that our minds can see more.

We need someone who paints life for us in calm colors and gives us glad tidings that life is not so cruel.

We need someone who hears us with his heart and then returns to being a stranger as he was.

We need someone to support us and support us even with a word.

We need someone to feel the whisper of our sorrows among the noise of our loud laughter.

We need someone to break down the wall of our loneliness, to make us feel that someone cares about us, even if they do nothing.

We may need love once, but we need safety and reassurance thousands of mirrors.

Why do you close the doors of awareness, love and beauty to yourself? If you want to get to the truth and the truth of your essence, just remove the illusion barrier and open the windows of your heart, soul and consciousness to the sun.

There is nothing in this world that can comfort or release a person from grief, inner weariness, or external difficulties.

Such as knowing the value of himself, his mission, purpose and quality. To realize that all the moments and people he missed are among the dead, and that his life is not in the past.

But here and now in the concrete situation in which he now finds himself.

Insight remains the strongest compass that guides you to the right path and inspires you to make the right decision.

Correct insight does not deceive its owner, does not mislead him, and does not waste him.

Insight is not about the laws of logic or reasons, it is about the light God casts into your heart, your feelings for those around you.

Therefore, whenever you want to strengthen your insight.

Make your heart purer for it to be well received, clean it of all that is negative so that can accommodate, and allow it to absorb this light until it is saturated with it.

We are so far away in terms of distance and miles, words can touch us and move us, thoughts can bring us smile. If yesterday was lost, then you have today in your hands and if today will gather its papers and leave.

You have tomorrow, do not be sad about yesterday for it will return, and do not regret today for its gone.

Dream of a brights sun beautiful tomorrow.

Consciousness always precedes knowledge. The conscious does not need to rely on science or wait for proof of science to confirm the truth of what he believes in. Rather, the truth is that science is discovered theoretically after it is reached by spiritual awareness first, and then science follows with proof and what is not proven does not mean it is wrong. Rather, it means that there are two cosmic possibilities and paths, one of which appeared with a yes and the other with a no.

Geniuses such as Da Vinci, Einstein, and Tesla when they reached what they reached first with spiritual knowledge or inspiration and imagination as in the expression of Einstein and Tesla, and then through that knowledge they try to find proof and theoretical scientific evidence for it so that people can accept it and believe it as a fact.

"I did not reach my understanding of the basic laws of the universe through my rational mind."

"The mind does not have much to do on the path of discovery. There is a leap in consciousness, call it intuition or whatever you want, the solution comes to you, and you do now know and why"? -Albert Einstein.

"The gift of mental strength comes from God and if we set our minds on this fact, we are attuned to this great power."

Be grateful for all the obstacles of life from the depth of yourself for them, and for their curses do not resist. It is only a stage of purification and cleansing of the impurities attached to the illusion of the mind, so be grateful.

It will open for us a thousand doors and doors and doors of grace, abundance, love and peace.

I am deeply grateful to her, and you are also grateful, because it is a message of love and upliftment. They called for the consciousness of a spirit and boundless blessings from God.

All love, peace.

If you are destined to fall in love with a "free" woman who has traveled many miles on her journey of liberation, you must know that the universe has chosen a journey for that is very different from what you thought you were going to. In this journey it does not matter if she shares the same feelings with you or not because she sees Love and need from a different perspective.

But in all cases, you are chosen and lucky, and this depends on the extent of your awareness, breath and desire to change yourself and love yourself with true love far from ego.

She will look like a woman that you have not looked at before, so every time an event will happen between you, you will see through her what you do not want to see and what must change and change in you.

Every time you stand by her words, something will vibrate inside you.

Sometimes it stirs anger in you, and another time it calms down and many times its swords will cause a revolution and a volcano in the depths of your soul, purifying everything. It calls for purification and moves what needs inspiration and courage.

if you were destined to fall in love with a woman who lived many lives within many family, emotional, human and spiritual experiences and repaired herself and transformed her pain into light and love, you must go through with her the pain that is a new birth for your soul and mind.

It will be like water that penetrates every part of your being, suddenly like a river that you cannot stop or prevent its influence on you. It is also like fire; you will not be able to prevent it from purifying you and turning your inner chaos and messing up your mind into ashes before your eyes.

She is also a light that will illuminate for you everything that has been darkened but beliefs, programs, ideas and duplicates.

It is like life, contradictory, changing, similar to the universe that is constantly changing to destroy in you everything you think is fixed and color your views with the colors of life.

She is like air; she will not allow you to touch her unless you become as strong and free from everything as she is.

Through it, and only you will continue to recognize yourself every time, every event, and every situation.

She will be free to make realize the true meaning of freedom in you.

Perhaps you will not be brave enough to accept it, perhaps your ego will not allow you to be grateful for it. Perhaps, you will not

be able to bear the image that it reflects of you every time, perhaps you need to run away from it.

And you may also choose to reach yourself through it.

In any case, it is the gift of the universe to you and your only inspiration on this trip, but you choose to run away from it or admit.

Awareness, female and power, energy and femininity.

Love is the highest meaning in existence.

Love is nothing but to throw a seed in arable land and continue to care for it and take care of it until the plant grows day after day before our eyes.

We have also tired of watering and caring for it with the water of kindness, attention, cooperation and appreciation. We do not skimp on it with any effort.

Today came the harvest of the plant, and it became a flower and I thought to add some beauty to it. I placed it in an elegant vase and a little water to keep it from wilting and to enjoy its sweet scent that perfumes the place.

The goal is that God bestowed upon us the grace of love, which is good. We must thank Him for his grace, nurture it, and preserve it so that it may continue and reap its fruits.

Good morning and light

Hungry Soul

Have you ever felt that you are hungry, and you cannot feel full, not only for food but emotionally hungry for relationships, financially hungry for gains, self-hungry for success and self-fulfillment. Hungry for fame and limelight, hungry for health and physical strength, hungry for religion ang religiosity and don't get satiated.

When the soul is hungry, only one thing will feed it. More hunger, how?

The hunger of the soul may be interpreted by our mind as worldly things. Eating, expanding the circle of acquaintances, entering romantic relationships, achieving sums of money and filling bank accounts with numbers and zeros, or practical success in a profession or craft. Rising to ranks of fame and attracting the attention and attention of people. Even with false success, going to health clubs, playing sports, trying to get fit and muscular. Sometimes by deadly means, joining groups whose motto is religions or speaking in the spirit of religion to touch the hearts of people. And I tell you that you will not be satisfied.

The hungry soul needs an awareness that is higher than the awareness of the mind. It needs the awareness of instinct, the awareness of being nourished by the presence of the Creator in it.

The feeling of safety and the feeling of heaven and light. Here it may calm down as there is no satiety from God's manifestation on the soul.

When you feel inner emptiness, emptiness and hunger, do not involve your mind in the interpretation because your mind will open the file of my worldly life for you.

When you go to him with your soul, ask Him to fill it for you with His presence. At that time, you will not feel hungry. For all that is less than God is greed and greed. He does not get fat and does not need hunger, and you will remain hungry for more?

Hunger is always not full of the presence of God. So, search within you. Have you diminished your resolve?

Has your passion and quest for God cooled within you?

Have you become satiated and obese from saturation with material things, fame, and relationships?

Have you been filled with them to the extent that they cut off the oxygen of life from you, and you have become choking in the slightest feeling?

Come back, fill your soul with it.

This fullness is the only satiety that will satisfy you. The more you feel that all life is sufficient besides God and Heaven are the goal.

They are the true craving that your soul seeks, and you do not know the explanation.

If you are not satisfied, go back to Him.

Invite Him to starve to Him. Ask that you starve with more passion and love in your quest for Him.

You will only be filled with Him, and you will not be satisfied until you meet Him and be content in His paradise, then you may be satiated.

The body is the mirror of the soul, and the soul is the mirror of feelings and feelings.

The mirror of thought and thought is the mirror of conviction, and conviction is the mirror of programming.

Have you noticed that convictions precede thinking, and this means that thinking will not change if convictions do not change?

It is impossible to make someone change without changing his conviction for him first, because he will not feel what you say of the positive, because you are unlike the frequency of broadcasting his negative convictions.

One of the wonders of convictions, even though it is programming.

"An unconscious program that was loaded in childhood in the unconscious mind." may kill its owner a thousand times a day.

What is even more amazing is that he is ready to defend it to the point of death, because deep down he does not understand it and does not realize the depth of it deadly influence on him.

Pay attention, convictions precede wisdom. So, it is difficult to judge and criticize them, as they move you with energy threads in the direction that you determine unconsciously and even attract through them events, circumstances, situations, and people of the same frequency, and you believe that all of this is coincidence.

Change your convictions, change your life.

Psychologically:

1. A house full of problems, tension, conflict and diseases is not the reason for magic, nor the jinn and goblins. The reason is the negative energy coming from their daily feelings towards each other.

2. One of the mistakes we make against ourselves is the endless postponements. We postpone thanksgiving, apologies, awareness, initiatives as if we are guaranteed to live long.

3. The man is the one who gives happiness to the family, and the woman is the one who gives love. The man cannot give happiness without love, and the woman cannot give love without being happy.

4. Some men want a woman who is; obedient but independent, jealous but understanding, foolish but kind, soft but strong. Their dream means a mentally ill woman but with schizophrenia.

5. The worst feeling is not knowing the reason for your anger and at the same time, you don't know what can satisfy you.

6. The more you scrutinize every issue in your life, the greater your psychological fatigue. That is why psychologists advise the importance of ignoring and underestimating things from time to time.

7. God will not forget your silence, nor the reproach you concealed, nor the oppression you brimmed with, nor the pain you endured, so trust in God and rest assured.

And never be afraid to start over, it's a new opportunity to rebuild what you want.

8. "If you want to pass a painful stage in your life, live it fully, do not be satisfied with neither anesthesia nor ignoring nor trickery nor half solutions alone confrontation will heal you"

Hand is Beautiful

Who always hold your hand,

And great are the words.

Who pats you on the shoulder, and does not wait for thanks, and the spirit is wonderful.

The one who embraces your soul and reassures her that she is her twin. Rare is the …

That spreads in your life the fragrance of happiness and interest without asking you for the price of perfume.

Peace be upon those who have the innocence of hearts, at the same time when sentiments are…

Peace be upon the pure good hearts that bear fruit,

Love and give us hope in life.

Peace to those who have the beauty of the soul and serenity, their hearts know nothing but loyalty.

The secret of the attractiveness of some is that he speaks to you with his spirit, not with his tongue, so he takes away your hearing, your heart, and your soul.

Certainty

Certainty is when you pray for something that everyone sees as impossible, but you raised your hands to the one who changes the laws of the universe by calling him.

Certainty is when armies of worries, anxieties, and anguish attack you, so you flee from it and hide behind both. Indeed, my Lord will guide me.

By God, if you want to remove a mountain from its place, then with certainty you can. Pay very close attention to what I am going to say. There is between supplication and receiving the answer, a time to test your certainty, patience, sincerity, and good faith.

By God, the answer is delayed, so you are in a test of your certainty, so be patient and God be patient and be certain of the answer.

Have you ever heard that God wastes deposits? Was it answered that God neglected his supplication? Is there a suffocating voice that ascended to God Almighty and returned disappointed? God forbid, so carry your wish and say, O God, I entrust my wish to you so keep it and do not look behind you.

Salvation is in the hands of the one with whom nothing is wasted. Do you know when a person recovers? If he approaches God, he approaches certainty.

Certainty that is not marred by doubt or objection.

Indeed, when God Almighty wants to bring you closer to Him closeness to the regulars not close to the common folk.

He will cut you off from your friends, family, and loved ones. Everyone abandons you and leaves you for no real reason, then he will send his armies against you, and the majority of your days and nights will prevail.

He will cut you off from the world and its sources, and your heart will cry out from the severity of what afflicts you until your breath becomes tight, and the simplicity is limited to dealing with you. Then the loneliness of creation increases in your heart, so you see them as your enemies.

"They are enemies to me except the Lord of the Worlds".

Then the sharpness of the severance between you and creation increases, and you drink from the cups of afflictions of all kinds and kinds until you see yourself as a stranger to everyone.

"Blessed are the strangers".

Then God will plunge you into the eye of the sea of loneliness.

You will see nothing but God, until the images of the universes are erased from your heart and leave all jealousy from your heart and reach the abstraction. Then he will push you into the singular, and the lights of God will descend upon you.

So be, "**to him, from him, by him, in him, to him**" then the phones of the truth call you.

"Indeed, I am God, Lord of the Worlds."

Then your closeness to him increases with the phone,

"And I chose you."

So, live by his prayers always, enjoying his monologues in the nights and days.

Then God will open for you what he wills of the treasures of knowledge and knowledge, and makes you an example for every guardian, righteous, and knowledgeable.

Until you leave the abode of the world and your body's cycle ends, and your soul remains in the world of isthmus, a grateful memory of God's blessings.

To wherever God, Lord of the worlds, wills.

O Allah, grant me and everyone who says, O Allah, Amen the ultimate pleasure of looking at your honorable face, the ultimate of your love, and the ultimate longing to meet you.

And the utmost of your love and the utmost longing to meet you.

Allah ou Akbarr

Who said thirst is only for water?

Sometimes, we are thirsty for a word the forces the mind and comforts the heart, or thirsty for a small spot that makes us feel safe in this world, or thirsty for some wellness, we are tired of sickness or thirsty for fulfillment, for gratitude, for the word thank you with love.

Then, I wish every first would be quenched by a glass of water words.

You are like a peg, one-third outward and two-thirds inward.

The law is to fix the outward part, and the truth is to fix the inward part, and the knowledge is revealed from the mixing of the two parts to fix the whole stake.

The truth is not only in visions and dreams, but rather in reforming the inner self and knowledge is the secret of wisdom, and wisdom is the secret of the idea.

And reform is the secret of the will of the aspirant, so there is no will without a will, and there is no will except by departing from the soul from all that is familiar to it and habit.

Your path does not stop except for you, and the sheikh is only a light to illuminate your path between your hands.

If the sheikh is absent, do not be absent from yourself, for the sheikh is nothing but supererogatory and you are your obligation.

The believer in the unseen without revealing is the one who is praise by God and the one who is given the provision of revealing.

Vision and dreams are not dignity, rather they are a sign on your path and a sign.

Praise be to God, Lord of the worlds.

The secret of the Soul.

If the negative thought is cut off from the flow of feeling, it disappears.

Thoughts feed on your feelings.

Feelings of importance, anxiety, and reinforcing the idea by believing it and raising its value. If an idea comes to the surface of your mind and you pay attention to it, this means that the ideas begin to lead you and separate you from yourself and rush you into a dark tunnel.

So, Eckhart Tolle says,

"You are not your thoughts."

The idea is something and you are something separate and completely devoid of everything around it.

An idea does not express your being, your identity, or your name. Imagine that you are a completely pure soul, she just observes everything around her with an eye of beauty and gratitude, without issuing its rulings.

Just watch and if encounter something annoying, negative news, an uncomfortable scene, a charged conversation.

All she had to do was look away calmly, at the other side. A soul that only has in its arsenal all the useful and enriching things and the deep that goes deep.

Freedom

Freedom begins with the mind, when you get rid of all those negative thoughts that keep you from moving forward and don't allow you to be free, we give space to our freedom.

And the most important kind of freedom is to be who you are.

Dare, live, love and enjoy each and every day, free yourself from all the thoughts that imprison you and do not allow you to be who you are.

The Fear

Fear can stop you from moving forward in life, but by facing it we can lead a full life, and I know it's not bad to feel afraid.

But the bad thing is to let fear control your life, because then you will have no life. You will only be afraid.

When we face our fears and overcome them, we will find freedom and a life of our own.

ABOUT THE AUTHOR

Thank you for your initial investment in getting acquainted with Alibaba, affectionately called Ali. The chosen name might initially mislead one's imagination or image, as Ali is a gentle giant of a man often overlooked by most. I recently visited the Giza Pyramids and discovered Ali diligently preparing breakfast for us at the local Great Pyramid Inn. (Regrettably, he no longer works there, a significant loss.)

Motivated to express gratitude, I offered a donation larger than the average for his services. This simple act revealed Ali as a person who opened himself up like a lotus, profoundly impacting my family's life. Acting as the caretaker of seven children under his roof, he goes out of his way to support his neighborhood, considering his friends as family. In a country with a for-pay healthcare system, where services must be paid for upfront, Ali stands as a pillar of his community.

Invited to his home, over the next four months, Ali shared beautiful words every day. Touched by his wisdom, I proposed printing these words into a book. Although he initially hesitated, citing a promise to God, Ali eventually agreed, open to seeing where my generosity and willingness to self-publish could lead.

All proceeds from the sale of these books will directly benefit Ali, his family, and his community, where he plays the role of a guardian or, as one might say, the real Godfather.

If you're open to experiencing people in their natural habitat, you'll discover that many individuals on this planet embody a loyalty to humanity that is often unseen. Perhaps by doing so, we can understand why we've been shaped to overlook the wonderful world around us, missing the chance to encounter grateful individuals who live life this way every day. Subhan Allah, which means giving thanks for what God has created. I run a nonprofit, Healing Space Presents, as a permission slip to sponsor such actions for others.

Join us in exploring the world, opening yourself to its numerous blessings!

P.S. Ali's wife, Jian Khatab, is possibly the best instructor for an authentic Arabic cuisine cooking class.

www.ingramcontent.com/pod-product-compliance
Lightning Source LLC
LaVergne TN
LVHW040200080526
838202LV00042B/3254